Star Friends

Night Shadows

D0980113

To Molly Tarris and Castaway, a very special horse,
who is cantering with the unicorns now—L.C.

To Jenny—L.F.

tiger tales

5 River Road, Suite 128, Wilton, CT 06897
Published in the United States 2021
Originally published in Great Britain 2018
by the Little Tiger Group
Text copyright © 2018 Linda Chapman
Illustrations copyright © 2018 Lucy Fleming
ISBN-13: 978-1-68010-481-3
ISBN-10: 1-68010-481-0
Printed in the USA
STP/4800/0459/1221
All rights reserved
4 6 8 10 9 7 5 3

www.tigertalesbooks.com

StarFriends
Night Shadows

BY LINDA CHAPMAN
ILLUSTRATED BY LUCY FLEMING

tiger tales

Contents

1
IN THE STAR WORLD

Millions of tiny stars shone in the velvet-black sky, casting a sparkling light over the mountains and valleys, forests, and lakes. In the woods, four of the wisest animals in the Star World had gathered around a forest pool—an owl, a wolf, an otter, and a badger. Their fur and feathers glittered with stardust, and their eyes were a deep indigo blue.

"How are the four young Star Animals who traveled to the human world to find Star Friends?" asked the badger.

"It must be three months now since they and their Star Friends stopped the elderly lady who was using dark magic," said the otter.

"Indeed it is." Hunter, the owl, touched the pool with the tip of his wing, and the water shimmered. "And Westport is peaceful again." A picture appeared in the water. It showed a pretty town with stone cottages, thatched roofs, and narrow streets. "The person using dark magic has forgotten all about magic, and the Star Friends have been using the magic current to help people," Hunter said. "Every good deed they do strengthens the current."

"Can we see the animals and their Star Friends?" asked the wolf eagerly.

Hunter nodded and swept his wing across the pool. The picture changed, showing four girls and four animals running into a clearing in the woods. The girls were laughing and the animals—a fox, a squirrel, a deer, and a wildcat—were bounding along beside them.

Behind the girls, a small waterfall splashed over gray rocks and flowed away in a stream that then ran through the trees down to the ocean. It was early spring, and the stream was swollen with rainwater.

"Mia, Violet, Sita, and Lexi," said the wolf softly, looking at each of the girls.

Mia, who had blond hair and sideways bangs, was chasing after the young fox, while Violet was stepping into a patch of shadows with the wildcat beside her. They vanished and reappeared on the other side of the clearing. Sita, who had long, dark hair and gentle brown eyes, spotted something in the grass and hurried over, with the deer trotting beside her. Crouching down, Sita picked up a baby bird that had fallen from its nest. She called to Lexi, who took the bird. Tucking it into a pocket of her coat, Lexi swung herself into a tree and climbed up to the bird's nest with Juniper, the red squirrel, next to her.

"They look very happy," the badger said contentedly.

But as the animals watched, a dark cloud began to swirl across the image.

The otter shifted his weight nervously. "What does this darkness mean, Hunter?"

The owl looked uneasy. "I think it is a warning to us that more evil is heading for the town."

"So soon?" said the badger.

Hunter nodded. "The clearing is a crossing place between our world and the human world, which makes it an area of very powerful magic. People who want to use magic for evil purposes will always be attracted to it."

The wolf padded around the pool. "I wish we could help."

"We cannot," said Hunter, a sad look in his round eyes. "We have had our time in the human world. It is up to the young Star Animals and their Star Friends to defeat this new threat."

"But what is it?" questioned the otter.

"I do not know," said Hunter, staring at the water. "Let us watch and see...."

2
SOMETHING STRANGE

Mia touched Bracken's rusty red fur. "Got you!"

The fox cub gave an excited yap as Mia raced away. She could feel magic tingling through her. When she connected with the current that flowed between the human world and the Star World, as Bracken had taught her, she could do all kinds of amazing things—see into the past, get glimpses of the future, and watch things that were happening elsewhere. Now, she used the magic to see where Bracken was going to move so she could dodge out of the way. She moved to the left, saw him start to jump that way, and dodged right at the last second, but Bracken knew her tricks well. He turned in the air and hit her chest with his front paws, sending her toppling to the ground.

"Got you back, Mia!" Bracken said, snuffling at her hair. She rolled him over, tickling the pale, downy fur on his tummy. He squirmed in delight, his bushy tail waving from side to side.

Mia felt a rush of happiness. She loved being a Star Friend! It was amazing being able to do magic with her three best friends and their Star Animals. The girls all had different magical abilities. Lexi could use magic to be incredibly fast and agile; Violet could travel to places using shadows, and make illusions appear; Sita could soothe and heal, and she also had the awesome ability to command anyone to do as she wanted—which, thankfully, she didn't use very often.

"Hey, guys!" Lexi called, sounded slightly anxious. "Come over here a minute." She jumped down from the tree.

"Did you put the baby bird back in the nest?" Mia asked, going over with Bracken.

Lexi nodded. "It's fine, but I noticed something strange while I was doing it." Her hazel eyes looked worried. Juniper leaped from the tree and landed lightly on her shoulder. His little paws played with the ends of her dark hair.

"What is it?" said Violet, appearing in the patch of shadows beside Lexi, with Sorrel next to her.

"The trees don't have any green spring buds anymore," Lexi said.

"That's weird," said Violet. "There are leaf buds on the trees outside my bedroom window at home, and there's even blossoms on the cherry tree in our front yard. I wonder why there aren't any spring buds here yet."

Juniper bobbed up and down on Lexi's shoulder, his red tail flicking around anxiously. "It's not that there aren't any *yet* but rather that the buds here are turning brown. They were green a week ago, but now they're all withering."

Mia realized something else that was odd. "There are usually spring flowers here in February. I used to come here with my grandma to pick daffodils and daisies."

"There *were* some daisies last week," said Sita. "I found a baby mouse near some." She went to the edge of the clearing. "Yes! Here!" She crouched down and then looked back over her shoulder in confusion. "They've died."

The others hurried over. The daisies by Sita's feet had shriveled up.

"This isn't good," said Sorrel, stalking around the brown clump of withered daisies, her whiskers quivering. "Trees and plants don't just die in early spring. I suspect dark magic must be going on here."

"Do you think it's someone conjuring Shades?" Sita said uneasily.

Shades were evil spirits who lived in the Shadow World. They could be conjured from the shadows by dark magic and then trapped in everyday objects. When those objects were placed in people's homes, the Shades began to cause misery and chaos. As Star Friends, it was the girls' job to work with their Star Animals to send Shades back to their own world. So far, the girls had fought a Mirror Shade who had been making Mia's older sister extremely jealous of her best friend; a Wish Shade who had made wishes come true in horrible ways; and four Fear Shades trapped in little yellow toy stretchy men who had terrified people.

"If someone is conjuring Shades, we'll stop them," said Violet determinedly.

A sharp thrill ran through Mia. Although fighting Shades was dangerous, it was also very exciting.

"Your bravery is admirable," Sorrel told Violet. "However, I cannot smell any Shades here."

"Neither can I," said Willow, her delicate nostrils flaring. Some Star Animals, like Sorrel and Willow, had a particular talent for smelling if Shades were near.

"So what's going on?" said Lexi, looking around.

"Remember, dark magic isn't just used for conjuring Shades," said Juniper.

"Yes, Aunt Carol used it to make that horrible snow globe," said Mia, petting Bracken and thinking of the elderly lady who had been using dark magic. She'd trapped Bracken and Willow inside a crystal globe. Mia would never forget how she had felt when she thought she would never see Bracken again. It had been the worst moment of her life.

"Indeed. You girls use the current of Star Magic when you do magic, but some people use the magic contained inside crystals or plants," Sorrel said. "Many people who use plants do good, but others perform very powerful dark magic by pulling the life force from plants and trees, leaving them dying." Sorrel touched the dead daisies with her nose. "It could explain what is happening in this clearing."

"How can we find out if that's what's going on?" Mia said.

Bracken put his paws up on her knees. "You could use your magic to see if anything strange has happened here in the last week."

"Go on, Mia," Violet urged.

Mia sat down on a tree stump. Pulling a small mirror out of her coat pocket, she looked into it. She needed a shiny surface if she wanted to use magic to see into the past or future. Cupping it in her hands, she let her mind open up to the current. Magic swirled into her, sparkling and tingling through her veins. "Show me if someone has been using dark magic here in the clearing," she said.

The surface of the mirror misted over for a moment, and then a picture formed. Mia was the only one who could see it, so she described it out loud. "I'm seeing the clearing at nighttime," she said. "Someone's coming into the clearing. They're wearing a long, dark coat with a hood. It's a woman, I think." The figure in the mirror looked around and then hurried to the center of the clearing, where she used liquid from a small bottle to mark a circle on the ground around herself. The circle lit up with a faint green light. The person corked the bottle and then put a silver bowl down in the center of the circle. She straightened up, showing a glimpse of blond hair.

"She's drawn a circle around herself with

some kind of potion," said Mia. "And now she's putting leaves into a metal bowl." She saw the woman wave her hand over the bowl and mutter some words. "It's like she's doing some sort of spell…." She gasped as the woman threw her arms in the air. The branches of the trees appeared to be pulled toward her as if by an invisible force. Wind whipped around the clearing, tossing her coat around her legs. The woman clasped her fingers together, and leaves suddenly exploded off the trees, flying high into the sky. The wind stopped and the trees' branches sagged, the buds shriveling. Around the woman, the leaves floated slowly to the ground like sad confetti.

"What can you see?" Violet asked impatiently.

Mia quickly told them. "Now she's picking up the bowl. The leaves have changed into a liquid. It's dark—almost black." She watched as the woman poured it into an empty bottle she took from her pocket and then stepped outside the circle. The light vanished, and she hurried away. "She's gone," Mia said slowly.

Sorrel hissed. "It seems someone has been doing dark magic here just as I suspected."

"But what for?" said Willow.

"And who is this woman?" said Bracken.

"I'll see if the magic will show me," said Mia. She looked into her mirror again. "Show me the face of the person doing dark magic," she said hopefully.

The hooded figure appeared in the mirror again, but her face was a blur. Mia shook her head. "She must be using a blocking spell to hide herself from anyone spying on her."

"We need to find out who she is," said Lexi.

"And stop her!" declared Violet.

Just then, Mia's phone rang, making them all jump. She checked the screen. "It's my mom."

"Where are you all?" her mom asked as she answered. "If you want to go to that new store in town before the movie, we need to leave Westport in five minutes."

"I'm sorry, Mom. We lost track of time. We're in the woods by Grandma Anne's house," Mia said.

"I'll drive to the top of the road," said her mom. "Meet me there in five."

"Okay." Mia clicked the phone off. "Mom says we need to go now."

The four girls had arranged a trip to the movies for the last afternoon of their February vacation.

"We'd better go and meet Mom," Mia told Bracken. "But I promise we'll try to find out who's doing dark magic here."

Bracken licked Mia's nose, and then he and the other animals disappeared in a swirl of starry light. They could vanish in an instant but would always reappear when the girls called their names.

The Star Friends took one last look around the clearing with its bare-branched trees and then hurried away down the overgrown path.

3
A CLUE?

The path came out on a little stony road. To the right, the road led down to the cliffs and ocean, and to the left, it led back up to the main road and town. Opposite the entrance to the path was a small house with a pretty yard and a little white front gate. Mia's heart twisted as she looked at it. It had been her grandma's home before she died, but now it had new owners.

The new family hadn't moved in right away. Painters and decorators had come and gone, and a patio had been quickly built onto the back. However, a few days ago, the moving vans had arrived. Now, a white van was parked outside the house, and a tall, slim woman, about Mia's mom's age, was directing two men as they carried some giant pot plants inside.

The lady smiled in greeting. "Hi, Mia!"

"Hi!" Mia called back. She had met the lady—Elizabeth—with her mom when she had come to look around the house. "Is the move going okay?"

"Yes, thank you. We're just about done. Can you tell your mom I'll stop over and have coffee with her soon?" Elizabeth said.

"I will! 'Bye!" Mia hurried after her friends.

"She seems nice," Sita said.

"Yes. She and Mom went to school together." Mia glanced at Lexi. "Your mom was with them, too."

Lexi nodded. "Mom said she knew her but they weren't really good friends."

"She has a daughter, doesn't she?" Violet said to Mia.

"Yes. I haven't met her, but she's starting at our school tomorrow. I think she's in fifth grade, like us."

"We'll have to help her settle in," said Sita. "I'd hate to start a new school in the middle of fifth grade."

Mrs. Greene—Mia's mom—was waiting at the top of the road in her car with the engine running. "Honestly, you girls," she said as they scrambled into the car. "We'd better get a move on or we won't get a chance to go to *Fairy Tales*."

"My sister, Simi, went on the first day it opened," said Sita. "She says they have all kinds of amazing stuff—models of fairies, elves, and unicorns, cards that can tell the future, jewelery, posters, and books."

"It sounds awesome." Mia remembered something. "Oh, Mom, we just saw Elizabeth. She said to say hi and that she'd stop over for coffee soon."

"Okay, great—it'll be good to catch up." Mrs. Greene shook her head. "It's funny how you can spend every day with people at school when you're younger, but then you all go your separate ways. I'd heard Elizabeth had started a business making herbal face creams and body lotions, but I didn't even know she'd gotten married and had a child until she came to look at the house."

Mia frowned, thinking that there was no way she would ever lose touch with Lexi, Sita, and Mia. "Why didn't you stay friends?"

Her mom shrugged. "We were in different friendship groups at school. Elizabeth was one of the popular girls. My friends were more into reading and studying."

Mia grinned. "So you were a geek, Mom!"

"There's nothing wrong with being a geek," Violet said.

"Nope. Geeks rule!" said Lexi. They high-fived each other. Both of them were very smart and always did well on tests and exams.

"Well said, girls," said Mrs. Greene approvingly. "Now, you'll all help Elizabeth's daughter, Lizzie, settle in, won't you?"

"Of course we will," Mia said.

"She'll either be with Mia and Violet in Miss Harris's class or in Mr. Neal's class with me and Lexi," Sita said. "So we'll be able to make sure she's okay."

Mrs. Greene smiled and drove on. When they got to town, they parked near the new store. It was tucked away down a little street with a cobbled alley on one side. It had a wooden sign with gold writing saying *Fairy Tales,* an old-fashioned front window, and a bell that rang as they walked inside. The air smelled of incense, and the wind chimes that hung from the ceiling were tinkling gently. The shelves were filled with fantasy figures and colorful packets of herbs.

A lady with shoulder-length blond hair was standing behind the counter. "Welcome to *Fairy Tales.*" She beamed. "I'm Alice. Let me know if I can help you."

"Thank you," Mia's mom said. "The girls
have been waiting to come in and take a look
around."

"Come in, dears," Alice said.

"Oh, wow," said Sita, heading over to a
shelf with unicorn models. "Look at these."

"Aren't these sweet, too?" said Lexi, picking
up a stone egg that had a dragon hatching out.

"Look with your eyes, not with your
hands," Alice trilled.

Lexi glanced at Mia. How old did Alice

think they were?

Mia's mom browsed some flyers while the girls looked around. "Oh, the Westport beachcomber sculpture competition," she said to Alice as she picked up a flyer. "We live in Westport, and it's always such a big thing. So many people enter—my next-door neighbor always makes something incredible and usually wins."

"I'm entering this year. I love collecting things from the beach and making things," said Alice. She winked at Mia. "And maybe the fairies in my yard will give me a helping hand!"

Mia smiled politely and escaped to join Violet, who was looking at a display of friendship bracelets with silver charms on them. "I like these—and look at those dreamcatchers." Violet pointed at the wall where some brightly colored turquoise, purple, and pink dreamcatchers were hanging. They were made with feathers and ribbon stitched onto a hoop. "They're beautiful."

"Hang one at the end of your bed, and they'll catch any bad dreams as you sleep," Alice called.

"How much are they?" Violet asked.

"Eight dollars each," said Alice. "But there are plenty of other cheaper things." She pointed to the shelf beneath the dreamcatchers. "There are some sleep-easy herbs and oils, or you could get a crystal. Crystals like rose quartz can bring good dreams, too."

Mia felt a chill run down her spine as she

looked at the crystals on display. Aunt Carol had used crystals to do dark magic.

"I don't think we'll buy a crystal," she said quickly. "Maybe a bracelet, though."

She got out her purse and bought a bracelet. Violet got one, too. Lexi bought a dragon egg, and Sita bought a unicorn, although she couldn't choose between them, so in the end Lexi chose for her—Sita was hopeless at making decisions.

"Okay, come on, girls," said Mrs. Greene, checking her watch. "We really have to go."

"How was the movie?" Mia's dad asked when Mia and her mom got home. He was in the kitchen making dinner with Cleo, Mia's fifteen-year-old sister. Max, their little brother, was playing with his trains on the table.

"It was good," Mia said. It had been a funny movie about animals on a rescue mission, but she had found it hard to concentrate because she kept thinking about the clearing. She really wanted to talk to Bracken, and she headed for the door.

"Wait a minute. Before you go, I saw this today." Mr. Greene held up a flyer. "There's a quiz at the village hall in a couple of weeks. I think we should enter as a family."

Cleo groaned. "A quiz? Do we have to, Dad?"

Her dad nodded. "It'll be fun to do something together. We might lose horribly, but who cares?"

"I think it's a great idea," agreed Mrs. Greene.

"If we're going to do something as a family, can't we just go to The Copper Kettle?" Mia said. It was the café in town, and she loved going there for a treat—the cupcakes were delicious!

"I think we should do something where we use our brains," her dad said. "It will be good for us!" He beamed.

Just then, Mia's mom's phone made a noise.

She checked it and sighed. "Ellie and Jo want to go for a run tonight. I suppose I'd better find my sneakers, although I'd rather have a cup of tea." She'd recently taken up running because she and her friends were entering a charity fun run, but she really didn't like it.

Mia slipped away to her bedroom.

"Bracken!" she whispered as she shut the door firmly behind her.

Bracken appeared in a haze of silver light and put his paws on her knees, his dark eyes shining with happiness at seeing her. "Did you have a good time?"

"It was okay," Mia said, petting him. "But I couldn't concentrate. I kept thinking about the clearing and the woman I saw doing dark magic there."

"I know," he said. "I wish we could find out who she is."

"I thought I might use my magic to see what's going to happen," said Mia. She'd been

thinking about it at the movie theater. Her
magic could give her a glimpse of the future and
might help them figure out what was going on.

"Try!" urged Bracken.

Mia sat down at her desk and looked into
the mirror there. "Show me what's coming,"
she whispered.

The surface swirled, and then pictures began
to flash across it: a hooded figure crouching
down in the clearing at dusk…. A wicker
basket filled with plants…. A collection of
small bottles filled with dark liquids…. A shelf
covered with crystals with a blur of bright
colors behind them….

The images faded.

"What did you see?" Bracken asked.

Mia frowned and described the pictures
she'd seen.

"You saw plants *and* crystals?" Bracken
said, his ears pricking. "Maybe the person
doing dark magic is using crystal magic as well

as plant magic."

"Hmm." There was something about the image of the shelf with crystals that was nagging at Mia. It had seemed very familiar. *Crystals…. Crystals….*

Suddenly, she gasped. "The crystals. They had dreamcatchers hanging behind them. They're in a store called *Fairy Tales* in town!"

"A store?" Bracken echoed.

"Yes, it's only been open a week."

Bracken bounced around. "A week? Mia, that's about when the clearing started to change. This could be a clue."

Mia stared at him. "The woman in there did seem odd. Maybe she's the person doing dark magic. I've got to tell the others!"

She pulled her phone out of her pocket and texted Violet, Sita, and Lexi. She wanted to tell them everything, but she knew she couldn't risk explaining in a text in case their parents checked their phones.

> Need to talk to u all. Meet b4 schl 2moro. I've seen something that might be VERY important! Don't be late! Mxx

She pressed Send.

"Done," she said to Bracken. "I'll talk to them tomorrow, and then we can all meet after school and figure out what to do." She hugged him tightly. "I hope this helps us find out what's going on!"

4
THE NEW GIRL

"What's up?" Lexi demanded the next morning. The four girls had run to a quiet corner of the playground where they could talk without being overheard. "I could hardly sleep last night. What's so important, Mia?"

"Yes, tell us!" Violet demanded.

Mia quickly explained about the shelf of crystals from *Fairy Tales*. "Maybe the person doing dark magic is using crystals as well as plant magic."

"And maybe it's Alice!" breathed Violet.

"I thought she seemed really nice," said Sita, looking troubled.

"We all thought Aunt Carol was nice, too, but she was doing dark magic and trying to hurt us," Violet reminded her.

"Alice could be just as bad as Aunt Carol," said Mia, excitement swirling in her tummy. "We need to find out more about her."

"Should we all meet after school?" Violet said.

"Yes. At my house," said Mia.

"I'll only be able to stay until five," said Lexi. "I have gymnastics, but I'll ask if I can come until then." Lexi and her sister did a lot of activities, and she found it harder than the others to meet up after school.

"Mia!" Mia heard her mom call. "I'm going now."

Mia ran over to say good-bye. As she did so, she saw a new girl coming onto the playground. She was very pretty, with her blond hair in a high ponytail, and she had lip gloss on. She was with a tall man with a bushy black beard.

"Do you think that's Lizzie?" Mia whispered to her mom.

Her mom did a double take. "It has to be," she said. "She looks just like Elizabeth when she was younger."

She went over to the man and girl. "Hi! I'm Nicky Greene, and this is my daughter, Mia."

Lizzie beamed. "Oh, hi. Mom said to look for you and Mia." She glanced at her dad, who hadn't said a word. "Say hi, Dad."

He nodded. His eyes were a very bright green. "Hello," he muttered into his beard. He seemed a bit odd.

"You can go home if you want, Dad," said Lizzie, giving him a little push. "I'll be fine." She looked at Mia. "You'll show me what to do, won't you, Mia?"

"Yes, sure," said Mia.

Lizzie's dad walked away. Mia stared after him. Weird! He hadn't even said good-bye!

"How are you feeling about starting here, Lizzie?" Mrs. Greene asked. "I imagine Westport Elementary will be very different from your school in Portland."

"It's a lot smaller," said Lizzie. She flicked her hair confidently over her shoulder as she looked around. "But I don't mind starting a new school. I'm sure I'm going to have fun!"

Mia introduced Lizzie to Violet, Lexi, and Sita. As Lizzie studied them, Mia saw her friends as they must appear to the new girl: Violet neat and tidy as always, her uniform and shoes sensible rather than fashionable, her strawberry-blond hair tied back in a ponytail.

Lexi loved clothes and was wearing a pretty red cardigan with her gray school skirt and shiny black shoes. Her dark curls were clipped back with a red barrette. Sita, on the other hand, wasn't into fashion at all and happily wore her sister's old school uniform. Mia wasn't sure if she imagined it, but she thought she saw a faint sneer on Lizzie's face as she took in Sita's faded sweatshirt and gray pants with paint stains on them.

"Do you know which class you're in?" Violet asked her.

"My teacher is Mr. Neal," said Lizzie.

"That means you'll be with me and Lexi," said Sita. "We'll help you out."

"Thanks," Lizzie said. She turned to Lexi and gave her a bright smile. "I like your bag."

Lexi smiled back. "I like yours, too." Lizzie had a black bag covered with red hearts. "And your shoes."

Lizzie put one foot next to Lexi's. "They're

very similar to yours, aren't they? Hey, do you want to swap phone numbers?" She pulled a shiny iPhone out of her pocket.

"Nice phone," said Lexi.

"Mom always gets me the latest model," said Lizzie airily.

"Well, if you don't want it confiscated, you'd better put it away," Violet said sharply. Mia glanced at her. Violet had no time for people who were into fashion and phones and stuff like that.

Lizzie looked surprised. "Really? Why?"

"We're not allowed to have phones at school. If the teachers see it, they'll take it from you," Mia explained. "Did your old school let you have them?"

"They did," Lizzie said slowly, "but I can see it's going to be different here." She put her phone into her bag. "It's going to take me a while to get used to the new rules."

Just then, the bell rang.

"Come on. Sita and I will show you where to line up," Lexi said.

"Okay. See you later, Mia," Lizzie said.

"See you!" Mia called, noticing that Lizzie hadn't said good-bye to Violet. From the way Violet's expression had tightened, it was clear she had noticed, too.

At recess, Lizzie and Lexi came out of their classroom together with Sita following behind them.

"How's it going?" Mia asked Lizzie.

"Great, thanks." Lizzie linked her arm through Lexi's. "Lexi's been so helpful."

"Mr. Neal asked me to be Lizzie's buddy," Lexi said.

"We're sitting next to each other," Lizzie said. "And we're doing a project on volcanoes together. We've got some great ideas for it already. Lexi's really clever," she said to the others.

Lexi looked happy.

Mia glanced at Sita. She was being very quiet. "Who are you doing a project with?" she asked her. Sita usually worked with Lexi.

"Jack," said Sita.

Mia gave her a sympathetic look. Jack was

loud and messed around.

"I think Jack likes Lizzie," Lexi said with a grin. "Tyler, too. They keep coming over and asking her if she needs anything."

Lizzie giggled. "They're both cute." She looked at Mia, Violet, and Sita. "Do you have boyfriends?"

"No," said Sita.

Violet rolled her eyes. "You're not one of those girls who just want to talk about boys, are you?"

Mia saw Lizzie's eyes narrow and felt a distinct chill fall.

"So what do you like doing, Lizzie?" she said quickly.

"Shopping and hanging out with friends," Lizzie said, turning her back on Violet. "I like inventing dances and watching videos about makeup."

"That sounds cool," Mia said, catching sight of Violet rolling her eyes.

Lizzie smiled at her. "You'll have to come over to my house. You, too, Lexi. Oh, look," she said suddenly. "Tara and Sadie are waving. I'm going to go and say hi. Catch you back in class, Lexi. 'Bye, Mia." She went over to where Tara and Sadie were. They were two of the prettiest and most popular girls in fifth grade.

"I don't like her," Violet said decisively.

"You just met her," Mia said, although she did kind of agree with Violet. She didn't like the way Lizzie had ignored Violet and Sita as she walked off.

"We should give her a chance," said Sita. "She may turn out to be nice."

Mia saw Violet open her mouth to argue. "Look, let's not waste recess talking about Lizzie," she said hastily. "We've got much more important things to discuss."

To her relief, the others nodded, and they headed off for their favorite quiet place on the playground. There was a grassy bank and a low wall to sit on.

"Have you thought about what I said this morning?" Mia whispered.

"I can't stop thinking about it," said Violet. "I think we should go to *Fairy Tales* after school and see if we can find out anything more."

"But how will we get into town?" Mia said.

Violet grinned and pushed back her strawberry-blond ponytail. "With magic, of course!"

5
SOME DETECTIVE WORK

When school was over, the four girls hurried back to Mia's house. As they arrived, they heard the sound of crying. Max was sitting on Cleo's knee in the kitchen. There were tears running down his face.

"What happened?" Mia asked.

Cleo sighed. "Mom asked me to babysit while she went for a run, and Max decided to see if Mr. Rabbit could fly. He threw him out of his bedroom window, and now he's stuck in the tree outside the window!"

"Oh, Max!" Mia groaned. Mr. Rabbit was Max's favorite cuddly toy. He couldn't sleep without him. "Want Mr. Rabbit!" Max's voice rose in a wail. "It's okay, Max. Dad will get a ladder and get him down from the tree when he comes home," said Cleo, smoothing her brother's hair.

"Want him now!" Max sobbed.

Mia glanced at Lexi. Could she help?

Lexi saw the look. "Let me see what I can do," she said. "I'm good at climbing."

"There's no way you can climb all the way up into the branches where he is," said Cleo.

But Lexi was already heading out of the French doors that led into the backyard.

Sita crouched down, taking Max's hands.

"Shh, Max, shh," she soothed. "It's going to be okay. You're going to get Mr. Rabbit back. Don't cry anymore."

Max's sobs dried to hiccups. Mia knew that Sita was using her calming powers. Max stared at Sita, his blue eyes wide. "Mr. Rabbit come back?" he said.

"Yes," she said.

He smiled.

"Here he is!" Lexi said breathlessly, appearing in the doorway a few minutes later with Max's cuddly rabbit in her hand.

Cleo gaped. "How did you get him?"

Lexi grinned. "I told you. I'm good at climbing." She kicked off her shoes and brought Mr. Rabbit over to Max. Max grabbed him and hugged him as if he was never going to let him go.

Mia smiled. She loved it when they were able to use magic to help solve little everyday problems and make people happier. She grabbed a sleeve of chocolate cookies. "Let's go to my room."

They hurried upstairs.

"Thanks for getting Max's rabbit," Mia said to Lexi as she shut her bedroom door.

"No prob. It was fun!" said Lexi. "You can see all kinds of stuff if you climb up trees. I saw your neighbor making a giant swan out of driftwood. He didn't see me, though."

"It must be for that beachcomber sculpture competition," said Mia. "He always wins." She opened the cookies and handed them out. "Now, let's get on with some more magic!"

They called the animals, who appeared and bounded around them in delight.

"Mia!" Bracken said, leaping into her arms and licking her neck. She hugged him tightly and buried her face in his soft fur. She missed him so much when she was at school. Next to her, her friends were greeting their animals with cuddles, too.

They all settled down, and the girls told
the animals the plan they had come up with.
They had decided that Violet and Mia would
shadow-travel to *Fairy Tales.* They would take
Sorrel with them and see if she could smell
any Shades. Lexi and Sita were going to stay
behind in Mia's room—Lexi had to be there
in case her mom arrived early to take her to
gymnastics, and Sita said she was happy to
stay and make an excuse if Mia's mom came
looking for them.

"I wish I could come with you," Bracken
said, sighing.

"I know, but people might wonder what was going on if wild animals like you or Willow or Juniper turned up in a store," she said.

"How will you take Sorrel inside?" said Willow. "People don't normally walk into stores with cats, do they?"

Mia grinned at Violet. "No, but we have an idea for that, too!"

Ten minutes later, Violet was holding a plastic pet carrier that Mia had brought in from the garage. Sorrel was inside it, the tip of her tabby tail quivering furiously. "I cannot believe I am doing this!" she hissed. "Imprisoned in a cage like a common housecat!"

"Sorrel, we've been through this," Violet soothed. "You just need to pretend to be a regular cat so we can get you into the store in this crate."

"And you're not really imprisoned," Mia

pointed out. "You could magic yourself out of there at any time."

Bracken pressed his nose against the wire-mesh door. "Be a good little kitty cat, Sorrel," he teased.

Sorrel swiped a paw at him, her claws clanging against the wire mesh. "Watch it, Fox!" she spat.

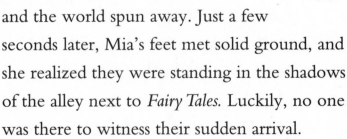

Bracken yapped as if he was laughing.

Violet glanced at Mia. "I think we'd better go!"

They stepped into the shadow of Mia's wardrobe, and the world spun away. Just a few seconds later, Mia's feet met solid ground, and she realized they were standing in the shadows of the alley next to *Fairy Tales*. Luckily, no one was there to witness their sudden arrival.

"Time to see what we can find out," said

Violet, her green eyes sparkling.

The girls pushed open the door to *Fairy Tales*.

"Hello again, dears," said Alice. She was putting out some new dreamcatchers behind the shelf of crystals.

"Do you mind if we bring my cat in?" said Violet. "We're on our way to the vet, but we really wanted to come in and take another look around."

Alice beamed. "No problem at all. I love animals."

The girls shut the door, and Alice put down the dreamcatchers and came over. "Who's a little cutie-pie?" she cooed to Sorrel in a high-pitched voice. "Who's a precious kitty cat?"

Sorrel hissed.

"Oh, dear. Someone isn't in a very good mood," said Alice. "Does the cat not like going to the vet?"

"No, she doesn't," said Violet hastily as Sorrel spat. "I'll just put her down here."

She placed the carrier on the floor near the shelf with crystals.

"So, what can I help you with today?" said Alice. "If you want a dreamcatcher, you'd better buy one fast. They're selling like hotcakes at the moment!"

"I just want to look at the bracelets again," Violet said. She and Mia pretended to examine the bracelets, glancing at Sorrel to see if she was showing any signs that she could smell Shades, but she had retreated to the back of the carrier, and all they could see was the tip of her tail.

Mia looked all around the rest of the shop, but there was nothing to suggest Alice was performing dark magic.

After five minutes, Violet bought another bracelet so that Alice wouldn't think it was strange that they were stopping in without buying anything. Then they left and hurried back into the alley.

"Well, did you smell any Shades in the

shop?" Violet asked Sorrel.

"No, I didn't, but I did feel magic in the air." Sorrel pressed her face to the mesh. "Now let me out of here!"

"As soon as we're back home," Violet promised, grabbing Mia's hand and stepping into the shadows.

When Mia, Violet, and Sorrel got back to Mia's bedroom, they let Sorrel out right away.

"Did you learn anything?" said Lexi.

"I learned that I do not like that woman who owns the store." Sorrel bristled. "Kitty cat indeed!" she huffed.

Bracken and Juniper snickered, and Sorrel glared at them.

"Stop it!" Willow told them. She blinked her large eyes at Sorrel. "It was very good of you, Sorrel, to put up with being in a cage just so we could find out more."

Sorrel looked slightly appeased.

"Did you smell any Shades there?" Sita asked.

Sorrel shook her head. "No. But I did sense magic in the shop."

"Dark magic?" said Mia.

"Just magic," Sorrel said, sitting down and wrapping her tail around her paws. "Our fur tingles when we are near magical objects or in places where magic is being used."

"So there was a feeling of magic, but Alice doesn't seem to be conjuring Shades," said Mia thoughtfully. "She's got to be doing something with the crystals, though, or why would the magic have shown them to me?" She rubbed her forehead. It was very confusing.

A knock on the bedroom door made them all jump. The animals vanished instantly.

Mrs. Greene stuck her head around the door. "Lexi, your mom's here."

Mia went downstairs with Lexi to say good-bye. Mrs. Thompson, Lexi's mom, was waiting in the hall.

"So how are things, Anna?" Mia's mom said.

"Very busy," Mrs. Thompson replied as Lexi put her shoes on. "I'm completely rushed off my feet."

"I don't know how you manage to work and fit in all the after-school activities," said Mrs. Greene. "Your girls do so many things. How do you do it?"

"With difficulty at times, but it's about looking to the future," Lexi's mom said. "If they want to go to a top university, then all the extras will help. It's a competitive world out there, Nicky."

Mrs. Greene laughed. "Oh, Anna. I can't believe you're thinking about college already. We've just decided which high school Mia's going to!"

Just then, there was a knock at the door.

Mia's mom opened the door. "Elizabeth!" she said in surprise, seeing Lizzie's mom on the doorstep.

"Hi. Is now a good time to have that cup of coffee?" said Elizabeth. She did a double take. "Anna! Gosh, I haven't seen you in years."

"I know. It must be twenty-five years," said Lexi's mom. "I heard you were moving back here. We'll have to catch up, but not now. Lexi has gymnastics."

"Another time, then," said Elizabeth.

Elizabeth watched as Lexi and her mom got into Lexi's mom's white sports car. "Anna looks like she's done well for herself," she commented.

"She's an accountant for a soft drink company," said Mia's mom.

"She was quiet as a mouse in school," said Elizabeth, a strange note in her voice. "I'd never have guessed she'd go on to be so successful. Sarah, too—I heard she's a doctor."

"Sadie's mom?" said Mrs. Greene. "Yes, she's a consultant at the hospital."

Elizabeth shook her head and turned to Mia. "Lizzie said you and Lexi were really friendly today. Thank you."

"No problem," Mia said.

"She's going to have a few people over tomorrow after school for pizza and a movie— and she wants you to come," Elizabeth said. She looked at Mrs. Greene a bit apologetically. "I know it's a school night, but Lizzie really wants to make friends. Are you free, Mia?"

Mia hesitated. She actually wanted to meet with Violet, Sita, and Lexi after school. They needed to find out more about Alice and the crystals. But her mom answered for her.

"That'd be fun, wouldn't it, Mia?"

"Yes. Thanks for inviting me," Mia said politely and then, leaving the moms to chat, she went upstairs to join the others.

Violet and Sita were cuddling Sorrel and Willow. Bracken bounded over to Mia as she shut the door. "We've been trying to figure out what to do next," he said.

"Do you have any ideas?" said Mia hopefully.

"We think we should go to the clearing and see if we can find any clues," said Violet. "And use magic to spy on Alice. How about we meet at my house tomorrow?"

"Can't." Mia sighed. She told them about the invite to Lizzie's. "She'll probably invite you two as well."

"I don't think she'll invite me," said Violet.

"Or me," said Sita. "I get the feeling she doesn't like me very much. I don't know why. I've tried to be friendly."

"I wouldn't worry," said Violet. "I think she only likes people who want to talk about boys and who don't have any brain cells."

"Thanks," Mia said, raising her eyebrows.

Violet grinned. "I didn't mean you or Lexi, of course."

"So let's meet on Wednesday after school and go to the clearing then," Mia said.

Violet nodded. "In the meantime, we can watch out for anything odd. If dark magic is being used, then bad things will soon start to happen."

Sita looked worried. "I hate the thought of Shades coming to Westport again and the plants in the clearing dying."

Mia nodded. "Don't worry. We'll figure out what's going on—and stop it!"

6
A NOT-SO-FUN TIME

"So this is the kitchen and this is the living room…." Lizzie gave a guided tour of her house the next day after school. As Violet had predicted, Lizzie had not invited her or Sita to come along, just Lexi, Mia, Tara, and Sadie. Both of Lizzie's parents were out. "They often leave me on my own," Lizzie said airily. "I don't mind, though."

Mia exchanged surprised looks with Lexi. Their parents never left them home alone. Even Cleo wasn't left for long. Mia followed the others. It was really odd being in her grandma's old house when it looked so different. The cozy clutter, flowery curtains, and old rugs had been replaced by white walls and wooden floors, slatted blinds, and leather chairs. There was a new back patio filled with lush plants and wicker furniture. And Elizabeth's office—once Grandma Anne's dining room—was filled with shelves of different pots and tubes of face and body cream, soap, and bath oil.

Lizzie's black cat lay on one of the chairs in the living room watching them.

Mia went to pet it, but it unsheathed its claws and glared at her in much the same way that Sorrel had glared at Alice. Mia hastily decided to leave it alone.

Upstairs, the four small bedrooms had been transformed into two large bedrooms. Lizzie's room had a double bed with a dark purple throw over the end and matching cushions, a white rug on the pale wooden floor, and sleek white furniture. There was a computer on the desk and a TV attached to the wall as well as a separate bathroom.

"Lucky! I can't believe you have a TV in your room," Tara said.

"I wish my bedroom was like this," said Sadie.

"It's perfect," said Lexi, looking around in awe. "You're so lucky."

Lizzie looked smug. She opened a cupboard and showed off an entire shelf of makeup and nail polishes, all in neat rows. "This is my makeup studio. We'll do each other's makeup later, and then I'll order a pizza for dinner."

"You're allowed to order food?" said Sadie.

Lizzie nodded. "Whenever I want."

Mia glanced at Lexi again. Lizzie seemed so grown up. She noticed a purple dreamcatcher hanging in the window and went over to take a look at it.

"Did you get this from *Fairy Tales?*" Mia asked Lizzie.

Lizzie nodded. "My mom bought it for me yesterday. It's nice, isn't it?"

"It's really pretty," said Sadie. "I wish I had one."

"Me, too," said Tara.

Lizzie smiled. "Well, luckily for you, I like to share things with my friends." She hurried

out and came back with four dreamcatchers
still in their plastic wrappers. "Here,
you can have one each."

"Really?" said Lexi.

Lizzie nodded and handed
them out. She gave pink
and turquoise ones to Mia,
Lexi, and Sadie and a purple
and red one to Tara.

"Why do you have so
many of them?" Tara asked.

"Mom likes to buy things
that she can use as birthday
presents," Lizzie said airily. "She
keeps them all in a big box in her
room. But she won't mind me giving these to
you. She's great like that."

"Wow, thanks!" said Sadie.

Lizzie beamed. "Now, should we do our
nails? I'll be the nail artist. You can choose
whatever you want."

They sat down in a circle, and Lizzie put some music on and began doing their nails. She was very good at it—she didn't smudge any of the nail polish or leave any blobs of it on their skin, but Mia found it very dull. Lizzie had some old books on her shelf that looked like they had probably belonged to her mom. Mia picked up one and started to read it while the others talked about makeup and the boys in class and the internet stars they liked. Mia tuned out their voices and let the story pull her in.

Suddenly, a hand slapped down on the book, knocking it out of her hands. Mia jumped. Lizzie was standing in front of her. "Don't be boring, Mia!"

Mia felt her temper prickle at Lizzie's bossy tone and the way she'd just knocked the book out of her hand, but she guessed she had been a little rude, reading and not joining in, and so she forced herself to smile. "I'm sorry."

"You're here to have fun, not to read," Lizzie said, picking up the book and throwing it to her. "You can borrow this if you want, but don't read it now."

Mia caught it and put it in her bag, feeling irritated but trying not to say anything.

Lizzie smiled at them all. "I think at school tomorrow we should have matching ponytails and hair clips." She pulled out a box of different hair clips. "I have plenty of red ones. Let's style the ponytails now and put the clips in. I'll do yours, Mia."

Mia reluctantly let Lizzie brush her hair into a high ponytail. "It has to be high," Lizzie told the others, pulling Mia's hair tightly as she held it above her head and twisted a band around it. "Low ponytails look so babyish."

"What, you mean like Sita's?" said Tara with a snicker.

Mia stiffened.

"Yeah. She should look in the mirror

sometimes." Lizzie laughed. "And have you seen how old her sweater is?"

"Her clothes are ugly," Sadie agreed.

Mia jumped to her feet, pulling away from Lizzie. "Stop being mean! Sita's our friend." She looked at Lexi, who nodded.

"Sita's really nice," Lexi said.

"So stop being horrible!" Mia said, glaring around.

Lizzie shrugged. "Chill. But if you're in *my* squad, you have to have a high ponytail!" She walked over and put a clip into Mia's hair, pushing it extra hard against her scalp and making Mia wince. "Okay, Lexi," she said brightly. "Let me do your hair, and then when we all have ponytails, I'll order the pizza, and we can watch a movie."

"Awesome!" said Sadie.

Lexi went over so Lizzie could do her hair. Mia folded her arms and sat down on the bed, wishing she was somewhere else. She had now decided she really didn't like Lizzie, and she certainly didn't want to be in her squad.

Even the pizza and large bottle of soda that Lizzie ordered wasn't enough to change Mia's mind, and she was very glad when her mom arrived to pick her up.

"I'll see you tomorrow in school," Lizzie said. "Remember your hair clip."

Mia had no intention of wearing it, so she didn't say anything.

"Did you have a nice time?" Mrs. Greene asked as they walked back to the car.

"Not really. I don't like Lizzie very much," Mia muttered.

Mrs. Greene looked surprised. "That's not like you, Mia. Don't judge her too quickly. Moving here will be a big change for her. You may not be seeing the real her at the moment."

Mia wasn't convinced. She was very relieved when they got home and she could talk to Bracken.

"How was it?" he asked.

She petted him. "Awful. I'd much rather have been meeting up with you and the other animals and Violet and Sita. Now we've wasted a day when we could have been trying to figure out what's going on."

Bracken climbed onto her knee and licked her cheek. "Don't worry. We'll go to the clearing tomorrow and see if we can find any clues then."

Her arms closed around his warm body, and her bad mood faded. Bracken was right. They'd only lost one day. "I love you," she told him. "You always make me feel better."

His eyes shone, and he snuggled closer. "I love you, too, Mia," he said.

7
Troubling Times

Mia was surprised when she got up and found her mom getting ready to go out for a run. "It's only seven o'clock!" Mia said.

Her mom nodded. "I know, but I had this weird dream last night. I was taking part in the fun run, and I actually finished first. Well, I woke up just wanting to go out running. I'm already faster than Ellie and Jo, even though they have done much more running than me. If I train a little more, I think I could do pretty well in this race."

Mia blinked. "But you hate running."

"I do, but it's good to push yourself," her mom said. "And every run I do means another guilt-free slice of cake at The Copper Kettle!"

"Can we go there soon?" said Mia.

Her mom smiled. "Sure. Now get some breakfast. Dad will take you to school today." She tied her sneakers and set off.

Mia got ready for school. She brushed her hair but left it loose on her shoulders rather than putting it in a ponytail, and she put the red hair clip in her bag.

When Lexi arrived at school, her hair was pulled into a tight, high ponytail with the red hair clip that Lizzie clipped into it. It looked a little odd because her hair was only shoulder-length, so her ponytail was very short.

"Why do you have your hair like that?" Violet said, frowning at her.

Lexi blushed. "I ... um, just wanted a change." She looked at Mia. "You don't have a ponytail."

Understanding dawned on Violet's face as Mia shook her head. "Oh, I get it! Lizzie told you to wear your hair in a particular way so that you become clones of her. That's it, isn't it?" She looked across the playground to where Tara and Sadie were greeting Lizzie. They all had matching high ponytails with red hair clips. "It is!" she said incredulously.

Mia sighed and nodded.

"Lexi! Mia!" Lizzie called, waving to them. "Over here!"

Lexi went over, but Mia didn't.

"Why aren't you joining in?" Violet said to her.

"I don't like Lizzie," Mia said.

"Why?" said Sita in surprise.

Mia just shrugged. She didn't want to tell Sita what Lizzie had said about her. "I just don't."

Lizzie came over. "Why are you hanging around here?" she said, ignoring Sita and Violet. "And where's your hair clip?"

Mia rummaged in her bag and pulled it out. "Here, you can have it back," she said. "I don't want to wear it."

Lizzie's eyes hardened. "Then you can't be in my squad."

Mia met Lizzie's gaze. She wasn't going to be bullied. "Fine."

Lizzie snatched the hair clip. "Your loss." She flicked her ponytail and flounced back to the others.

"Why *does* Lexi like her?" said Violet in astonishment.

Mia shook her head. "I have no idea."

Lexi continued to hang around with Lizzie all day. Mia found it hard to understand. Yes, Lizzie was grown up and funny in some ways, but she was also mean.

At the end of the day, Lexi came out with Lizzie and the others. Lizzie was imitating Mr. Neal, and they were all giggling.

"Lexi!" Mia called. "We're going!"

Lexi said good-bye to Lizzie and ran over. "Lizzie's so much fun," she said.

"Really?" Violet said disbelievingly.

"You didn't seriously enjoy last night at her house, did you?" Mia said. "All that showing off and talking about makeup and boys?"

"Yes, I did enjoy it," said Lexi in surprise. "Well, most of it. Didn't you?"

"No," Mia said.

"Lexi!" They looked around. It was Lexi's mom. "Change of plan. You can't go to Violet's tonight, I'm afraid," she said, coming over. "I'm sorry, Violet."

"But why? You said I could go until my swimming lesson, Mom," said Lexi.

"I know, but when I woke up this morning, I realized that you could be using this hour and a half more usefully," said her mom. "I think it would be a really good idea for you to learn German, and I found a tutor who can fit you in on Wednesdays."

Lexi's face fell. "Mom! I already do French plus extra math, piano, tennis, gymnastics, and trampolining."

"Yes, and now you'll be doing German and flute, too," said her mom.

"But I won't have time to see my friends!" Lexi protested.

"You'll still have a few hours free on the weekend," said her mom. "Now come along. No arguing."

Shooting a despairing look at the others, Lexi went with her mom.

"Poor Lexi," Mia said, the irritation she'd been feeling with her friend fading instantly.

"I'd hate to have all those extra classes," said Violet.

"I'll stop over this evening and tell her what we've been doing so she doesn't feel left out," said Sita.

They headed back to Violet's house, dumped their school bags, and went to the clearing.

"Look at it!" Sita whispered, staring around horrified.

The clearing looked much worse than it had a few days before. A dark mold was creeping up the tree trunks, and even the evergreen trees had lost their needles. The leaves on the dark green ivy had turned brown, and the air smelled of dampness and decay.

"It's awful," Mia said. "What could have made it get so bad?"

"Dark magic," said Violet grimly. "Let's call the animals."

They called their animals' names. When Sorrel appeared, she hissed, her tail puffing up. Willow's nostrils flared.

"What is it?" Sita said in alarm.

"Shades!" said Willow, her eyes wide. "Shades have been here! I can smell them!"

8
STRANGE HAPPENINGS

"The air absolutely stinks of Shades," said Sorrel, prowling around the decaying clearing.

Bracken looked uneasy. "I can't smell Shades like you," he said, "but I can tell the clearing feels wrong. The air feels heavy and dull."

"The life force is being sucked out of it," said Sorrel. She looked around. "Where are Lexi and Juniper?"

"Lexi had to go with her mom," said Mia.

"I don't like it here anymore," said Willow, pushing against Sita's leg. "Can we go somewhere else to talk?"

Bracken nodded.

"Let's go to the beach," Mia said.

They set off through the trees. The animals kept to the shadows and then vanished when they reached the clifftop, only reappearing when the girls found a sheltered spot to sit down.

The beach was made of pebbles with big boulders at the bottom of the cliffs. They found a place where the boulders made a complete circle with dry pebbles in the center of them. There was no one anywhere nearby, just a few dog walkers and beachcombers in the distance. Overhead, seagulls screeched across the sky.

"What are we going to do about the clearing?" said Sita.

"I'll use my magic," said Mia. She took her mirror out of her pocket. "Show me who has been conjuring Shades."

The mirror swirled, but no picture formed.

"I'm not seeing anything," Mia said.

"Try asking something else," urged Sorrel.

Mia thought for a moment. "Show me where the Shades are," she tried.

But once again, the mirror showed nothing.

She bit her lip. "Show me what's coming," she said.

This time, an image did appear. It was followed by another and another: the same hooded figure in the clearing; a row of glass bottles filled with dark liquid.... Mia blinked.... A girl with her face buried in her hands, sobbing in a bedroom; a woman with

a hammer; Mia's dad shouting angrily …
and then a Shade's evil face suddenly filled
the mirror, grotesque and large, its red eyes
gleaming. "We are here!" it hissed. "Beware!
We three shall not be beaten!" Mia gasped and
dropped the mirror onto her knees.

"What is it?" Bracken said.

Heart racing, Mia described what she had
seen.

"It said there were *three* Shades?" said Sita
anxiously.

Mia nodded. Sorrel gave a hiss and paced
around the circle of rocks behind them. "This
is not good."

Sita looked anxiously at Willow. "Will the
things Mia saw definitely come true?"

"Not definitely," Willow said. "The magic
shows possible future events, but all of those
things can be changed."

"If we can figure out what's going on," said
Mia.

"You said you saw the figure in the woods again," said Violet, her face frowning in concentration. "Did it look like it might be Alice?"

Mia nodded. "It could have been." The person was about the same size and height as Alice.

"I bet it's her. Why else would the magic have shown you the crystals in the shop? Try spying on her," said Violet. "Let's see if we can find out anything more about her."

"I want to see Alice," Mia told the mirror.

She expected to see Alice in the shop and was surprised to see a beach appear in the mirror. Alice was walking along it with a bag over her arm. She was heading for a circle of boulders by the cliffs. Mia looked up in surprise. "I think she's here!"

She jumped up and went out through the boulders onto the pebbles and saw Alice walking toward them. "It *is* her!" she squeaked. The animals vanished, and Violet and Sita joined Mia.

"Hello!" Alice said, spotting them. "What a surprise to see you girls."

"A-and you," stammered Mia. She stared at Alice. Could she really be the person doing dark magic and conjuring Shades?

"What are you doing here?" said Violet suspiciously.

"Oh, it's half-day closing at the store today, so I thought I'd collect some bits and pieces from the beach for the beachcomber sculpture competition," said Alice. "I also wanted to gather some plants and herbs in the woods." She nodded to the bag on her arm.

"Plants?" Sita echoed.

"Plants can be used for magic, you know."
Alice's eyes twinkled. "You can make a sleep-
easy potion with lavender or a calming potion
with camomile. There are all kinds of magical
things you can do with plants." She tapped
her nose. "Believe in magic, dears. Remember
that. Now, I'd better go. My parking meter
is going to run out. See you in the store
soon, I hope—or maybe at the sculpture
competition!" She headed off down the beach.

The girls watched her go and then
disappeared back between the rocks. "We
were right!" Mia hissed. "She *is* the person
we're looking for!"

"She even just told us she uses plant magic!"
said Sita.

"Wait a sec!" said Violet, shaking her head.
"Something about this doesn't make sense."

"What?" said Mia impatiently.

"Would she really talk about magic so

openly if she's actually doing dark magic?"
Violet pointed out. "Wouldn't she want to
keep it secret?"

There was a pause as her words sank in.

"I guess it is a bit odd," Mia admitted.

"Hmm," said Sita. "Why would she tell us
she can do magic?"

"You know, I'm not sure about this
anymore," Violet said. "Maybe it's not her."

"But why did the magic show me the crystals
on the shelf at *Fairy Tales*, then?" said Mia.

"And if Alice isn't the person doing dark
magic, then who is?" said Sita.

They stared at each other, puzzled. None of
them had an answer to that.

When Mia got home, her dad was sitting at his
laptop at the kitchen table.

"What's for dinner?" Mia asked.

"I don't know," he said vaguely. "Mom's out

running, and I've been too busy to think about it."

"What are you doing?" Mia asked curiously.

"Putting together some quiz-team practice questions," her dad said enthusiastically. "I think we could do well in this quiz. We need to get practicing, though, to make sure we have the best chance of beating the other teams."

"Practicing?" Mia echoed.

"Yes, tomorrow night after school."

"But I'm meeting the others then," Mia protested.

Her dad shook his head. "Not tomorrow. We're going to practice. We could win this, Mia."

Cleo came in with a piece of mangled toast. "I just found Max trying to put this in the DVD player, Dad."

Mia expected their dad to rush into the living room, but he just waved a hand. "Can you deal with it? I'm busy with these quiz questions."

Cleo groaned. "Dad, it's just a little quiz in the village hall. It's not *a big deal*."

"Mmm." Her dad stared at the screen.

Cleo shook her head at Mia. "Will you help me? Max is very sticky—and so is the DVD player."

"Sure." Wondering why her dad was so obsessed with the quiz, Mia helped Cleo clean up Max and the DVD player, then pulled out her phone and texted Lexi.

Did u see Sita? Did she stop over?

A text came back from Lexi.

Mom wdn't let her in. She's making me do a practice math exam! Sita's going to call me later. Can't stop now. Gotta finish this math. Ugh!

Mia shook her head. Okay, her dad might be being a little weird, but Lexi's mom was a lot worse. Frustration welled up inside her. There were Shades in Westport. They didn't have time to do things like math papers and quiz practice. They needed to be doing magic! She remembered the Shade's gloating face and lifted her chin.

We'll stop you, she vowed. *Just you wait and see.*

"Come over in the morning, and we can hang out all day."

"Count me in," said Sadie with feeling. "My mom just told me she wants me to spend Saturday morning on the beach helping her find things to add to her beach sculpture for that competition thing. No. Thank. You."

"I can't come over first thing. I've got gymnastics," said Lexi.

"Come afterward, then," Lizzie said.

"Lexi always meets me, Sita, and Violet after gymnastics on Saturdays," Mia put in.

It was as if she hadn't spoken. Lizzie's eyes didn't flicker from Lexi's face. "You do want to be my friend, don't you, Lexi?" she said. Her voice sounded sweet, but there was a knife-sharp edge to it.

"Yes, of course!" Lexi said.

"Then you'll come to my house," said Lizzie with a confident smile. "Now," she hooked her arm through Lexi's, "let's go and

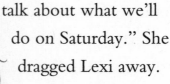

talk about what we'll do on Saturday." She dragged Lexi away.

Lexi gave Mia an apologetic look over her shoulder. Mia felt a rush of anger and marched onto the playground.

"Are you okay?" Sita said, seeing her face.

Mia shook her head. "No! I was talking to Lexi when Lizzie came along, and then Lexi went off with her. I think she might even be going to Lizzie's on Saturday after gymnastics rather than meeting up with us. I can't believe it!"

Violet's mouth fell open. "But we *have* to meet then! There's so much we need to do."

"I know!" Mia exclaimed.

"Lexi won't let us down," said Sita quickly.

"She'll meet us. I'm sure she will."

"Hmm." Mia wasn't convinced.

Cleo was making a sandwich when Mia got home that afternoon. "How was school today?"

"Okay, I guess." Mia shrugged.

Cleo frowned. "What's up?"

Mia poured herself a glass of juice from the fridge. Cleo could be annoying, but she was usually pretty good when it came to advice about friends. "It's Lexi," she admitted. "She's hanging around with this new girl, Lizzie, and the other popular girls in fifth grade. I don't get it. All they're into is boys and makeup and stuff like that."

Cleo shrugged. "Maybe Lexi's into that, too, now that she's getting older. People change in fifth grade and start to like different things."

"Not me and my friends," said Mia.

"It sounds like Lexi is into that. It's really

very normal. I wouldn't stress about it." Cleo stretched. "So what time do you think Dad wants to do this practice?"

"I don't know, but I hope he doesn't make us practice for too long." Mia sighed.

She went upstairs. Lying on her bed with Bracken, she cuddled him and told him about her day.

"Lizzie sounds horrible," he said, snuffling her neck. "Lexi is being silly. You're a million times nicer."

Mia smiled. Bracken always understood. "I'm glad I've got you, Bracken."

He snuggled closer and tipped his head to one side. "Could Lexi be behaving strangely and wanting to be this girl's friend because of a Shade?"

Mia had been wondering that, too. "I don't know. I don't really think so. She's not being mean or horrible or anything like that. She just likes hanging around with Lizzie, and Cleo told me it's normal for people to change in fifth grade."

"It might be worth getting Sorrel or Willow to check Lexi's house for Shades, though," said Bracken. "Just in case."

Mia nodded. "Good plan. Well, that's if Lexi's mom ever lets us in!"

"Mia!" her dad called. "Time to do some quiz practice!"

Mia kissed Bracken on the nose. "I'd better go. See you later," she said, and then she went reluctantly downstairs.

The quiz practice was not fun. Mia's dad kept going over and over the general knowledge questions until Mia was so bored that she thought she might explode.

Even worse, he then insisted on yet another practice on Friday right after school, which meant Mia wasn't able to meet up with Violet and Sita. Mia had never known him act like this before. She thought about the image she'd seen of her dad when she'd been using magic. He'd been shouting at someone. Could it have something to do with this quiz?

On Saturday, Mia got up and found her dad in the kitchen surrounded by cups of half-drunk coffee. He was reading over fresh question sheets he'd printed off the internet.

Mia got herself a bowl of cereal. She was just about to pour the milk when there was a knock at the front door.

Her dad answered it.

Hearing him talking to someone, Mia went

through to the hall. It was
their elderly neighbor,
Mr. Jones. He looked
very upset. "You didn't
hear anything then,
David?" he was saying
to Mia's dad. "It must
have happened between
midnight and six o'clock
this morning. I can't
believe it. After all the work
I put in."

"What happened?" Mia asked
curiously.

Her dad looked shocked. "You know the
sculpture Mr. Jones has been making for the
competition?"

Mia nodded. Mr. Jones usually won, and
this year, she knew he had been making a
beautiful swan out of driftwood and sea glass.
She'd seen it from her bedroom window.

"Someone went into his yard and destroyed it during the night!" her dad said.

"That's awful!" gasped Mia.

"They just smashed it up," said Mr. Jones, shaking his head. "The judging is this afternoon, so I can't make another one. I mean, who would do something like that? I spent hours making it."

"Did you hear anything outside, Mia?" her dad asked.

"No."

"I'll go and see if Pete and Doreen on the other side noticed anything," said Mr. Jones.

Mia hurried upstairs, her breakfast forgotten. Maybe she could use magic to find out who had damaged the sculpture! Shutting her bedroom door, she sat down at her desk and looked into the mirror. She breathed deeply, and magic swirled into her, warm and tingly.

"Show me what happened to Mr. Jones's sculpture," she said.

An image appeared of the yard next door
in the pale gray light of dawn. The beautiful
swan sculpture was on the picnic table.
Someone opened the gate and came in. Who
was it? To Mia's surprise, she saw a short,
dark-haired woman. Mia frowned. She was
sure it was a mom she recognized from the
playground, although she wasn't quite sure
whose mom she was. In shock, she watched
as the woman pulled out a hammer from
under her coat.

Mia's eyes widened. No! She'd seen this
before! It was the woman she'd seen when
she'd asked the magic to show
her the future!

"I *will* win!" the
woman muttered, and
then she started hitting
the delicate sculpture
with the hammer.
It broke into pieces.

She glanced around swiftly and then tucked the hammer back under her coat and hurried out of the gate.

Mia wondered what she should do. She couldn't tell Mr. Jones what she knew—she didn't have any proof he would believe her. For a second, she wondered if the woman could be the person doing dark magic in the clearing, but she was too short, and her hair was brown. It was much more likely that she was being affected by one of the Shades they knew were in Westport. Why else would she just attack the sculpture? Mia had never heard about her being mean or horrible before.

Mia took a deep breath. She had to tell the others so they could try and find out more. It looked like it was going to be a very exciting day!

10
THE WORK OF SHADES?

Mia went downstairs. Her mom was talking to her dad in the hall. "Ellie's out of the race! She's hurt her ankle," she was saying.

"Mmm," Mr. Greene said, hardly listening as he leaned against the wall, reading quiz papers.

"Mom!" Mia said, shocked. "You sound almost happy that Ellie hurt herself."

"Well, it means one less person to beat!" her mom said. A strange greedy look crossed her face. "Imagine if more people got injured. That would be good."

"What?" Mia stared. Her mom would never usually say something so mean.

"Just saying," her mom said with a sly smile. "I'd be more likely to win."

Mia edged away. This wasn't right. Why was her mom acting like this?

Shade! her mind screamed at her. It seemed the only possible explanation for her mom's odd behavior.

Mia's throat felt dry. Could there be a Shade in *her* house?

"I'm going out," she said suddenly.

Her dad looked up. "You can't. You need to study for this quiz!"

"But I'm going to Violet's," Mia said.

"No!" her dad's voice rose angrily. "You have to stay! You can't go out!"

Mia's heart flipped. What was going on? Her dad never shouted! It was just as she'd seen in the mirror!

"Stay here!" he yelled.

Mia didn't listen. She dashed to the front door and was through it and out before he could stop her. "See you later!" she gasped, and then she set off, running down the road.

By the time she reached Violet's, she was pink in the face and gasping for breath.

"Are you okay?" Violet said, coming to the door with Sita.

"No…," panted Mia. "Mom…. Dad…. Shades."

Violet and Sita gave each other alarmed looks. "Let's go upstairs," Violet said quickly.

They hurried to Violet's room. "Lexi texted this morning—she'll be here soon," said Violet.

"What happened, Mia?" Sita said.

"Call the animals first," said Mia.

Bracken sensed that there was something wrong as soon as he appeared. "What's the matter?" he said, bounding anxiously over to Mia. "You don't look happy."

Mia told them what had happened that morning. "I thought Mom and Dad were just being a little weird, but now I'm sure they're being affected by Shades. And that woman I saw who smashed up Mr. Jones's sculpture. Why would she do something like that? Maybe she did it because of a Shade, too."

"So we're dealing with a type of Shade that only affects adults by the looks of it," said Sorrel. "A Shade that makes people want to win and beat others."

"At all costs," said Mia with a shudder, thinking of the woman with the hammer and the creepy look in her mom's eyes as she had talked about people getting injured. "We have to find where the Shades are." She ran a hand through her hair. Three Shades—one in her house, maybe one in the woman's house, and then one somewhere else.

"Should we go back to your house?" said Bracken.

Mia hesitated. "I don't know. Dad was really mad. He might try to lock me in."

"Well, why don't we go to the sculpture competition instead?" said Violet. "It's being judged this afternoon in the beach parking lot. I bet the woman who destroyed Mr. Jones's sculpture will be there. We might find something out from her. Come on. They'll be setting up now." She jumped to her feet.

"Shouldn't we wait for Lexi?" said Sita. Her phone buzzed. "Oh, it's from her." Sita held out her phone, and they all read Lexi's message.

Can't come over now

"That's it?" Violet exclaimed. "That's all we get?"

"I bet she's gone to Lizzie's!" said Mia. Anger flashed through her. There wasn't a kiss or an emoji with the text. There certainly wasn't an explanation. How could Lexi let them down like this? They needed her—really needed her.

"She says she can't come over *now*," said Sita hopefully. "That might mean she'll come over in a little while. Let's wait a little longer."

Mia and Violet reluctantly agreed, but when Lexi hadn't appeared after another twenty minutes, Mia jumped to her feet.

"This is silly," she said. "We can't just sit around all day. She's obviously not coming."

Violet nodded. "I think we should go."

"Okay," Sita sighed.

They headed out of the house and down the street. There was music coming from the open windows of Lizzie's house as they walked past. "I wish Lizzie had never moved in," Mia muttered, thinking of Lexi inside. How could she abandon them to be with Lizzie and the others?

Just as they reached the clifftop, they heard a voice calling their names. They looked around and saw Lexi jogging down the street toward them. "I'm sorry I couldn't meet you earlier," she panted as she reached them. "Did you get my message?"

"Yes," Mia said shortly.

Violet folded her arms. "So you saw us passing Lizzie's house and thought you might finally come and join us?"

Lexi frowned. "What?"

Mia lost her temper. "I can't believe you dumped us to go and hang around with her! We've had enough, Lexi. You can't be friends with her and us—you're going to have to choose!"

"I didn't dump you!" Lexi protested. "I came

right from the new German lessons my mom is making me do. I tried to send a message telling you I'd be another thirty minutes, but before I could finish it, Mom took my phone away from me." She glared at them. "Did you really think I'd go over to Lizzie's rather than come and do magic when there's important stuff happening, stuff we need to deal with?" Her voice rose. "And even if you did think that, who are you to tell me who I can and can't be friends with?"

"Lexi, we're sorry." Sita stepped toward her while Violet and Mia stared open-mouthed.

"No. Don't use your magic on me, Sita!" Lexi snapped. "I've changed my mind. I don't want to be with you this afternoon, after all! I'm going home!" Turning, she ran back up the street.

"Wait!" Mia shouted, racing after her, but Lexi used her magic and vanished in the blink of an eye. Mia stared at the empty space where Lexi had been standing and then turned around. Sita was biting her lip and trying not to cry.

"Oh, dear. I think we owe her an apology," Violet said slowly.

Mia nodded. Her anger had disappeared as quickly as it had blown up, and now she just felt awful.

"Should we go after her?" Sita said.

"We'll never catch her if she's using her magic," said Mia.

"I could shadow-travel us to her house," said Violet.

"I don't know. Maybe we should give her some space," said Mia doubtfully, remembering how angry Lexi had been. When Lexi got upset, she tended to stay upset for a long time. She pulled out her phone and texted her instead.

> We're really sorry. Can we come over?
> Mxxxxxxx

"Let's wait to get a reply," she said.

Sita nodded. "I think that's best."

"Let's go to the competition for now," said Violet. "Hopefully she'll text us back soon."

They reached the clifftop. From there a walkway led down to the beach. On one side of it was a small parking lot. Usually in February there were only a few cars, but today it was packed with vehicles. There was a big canvas sign stretched across the entrance saying *Westport Beachcomber Sculpture Competition* in large letters, and tables were set up around the parking lot where competitors were laying out the sculptures they had made from things they had found on the beach. Another sign announced that the judging would begin at 2 p.m.

Mia looked around at all the people—some were drinking coffee, others were chatting or wandering from table to table admiring the sculptures. She nudged Violet and Mia. "There's Alice," she whispered, seeing the store owner fussing around her entry—a beautiful driftwood dragon with green seaglass for eyes and shells for scales.

"Should we go over?" Violet whispered. "We have to find out if she knows about the Shades or not."

"How do we do that?" said Mia.

"I know!" said Sita, suddenly looking determined. "It's time to sort this out once and for all. Follow me."

Mia and Violet exchanged surprised looks. It wasn't like Sita to lead the way, but they followed her over to Alice's table.

Alice beamed at them. "Hello, dears. Have you been taking a look around? Aren't the other entries amazing?"

"Yours is really good, too," said Mia politely. "I really like the—"

"Alice, I need to talk to you," Sita interrupted, her hazel eyes serious. She dropped her voice. "Now, you must listen to me and answer with the truth."

Mia gaped. She knew Sita was using her ability to command people to do anything she wanted. She also knew that Sita hated using that power.

Alice blinked. "I will," she said obediently.

Sita stepped closer. "Have you been using dark magic?" she asked.

Mia glanced around. Luckily everyone nearby was busy, and no one was listening.

Alice looked confused. "Dark magic? No. Just good magic. Sleep-easy potions, energizing oils, healing creams. I collect herbs. I make potions. People buy them, and they help."

The girls exchanged looks. So Sorrel had been right when she said she felt magic in the store. But someone else was responsible for the dark magic in the clearing.

"When I snap my fingers, you won't have to answer my questions anymore," said Sita. "And you will forget what I have just been doing."

Alice nodded. "I will forget," she repeated.

Sita snapped her fingers. Alice's face cleared. She looked confused for a second. "I'm sorry, dear," she said, shaking her head. "Did you just ask me a question?"

"I just asked how long it took you to make the dragon," Sita said. "He's great."

"Thank you. I've been working on him for weeks," said Alice.

"Good luck," said Mia.

"Thank you, dear," trilled Alice.

They moved away. They couldn't talk about what had just happened with so many people around, but Mia was sure the others were thinking the same thing as her. If Alice wasn't doing dark magic, who was? Suddenly, she caught sight of a short, dark-haired woman. She had a messy sculpture of a house on the table, and she was glaring around at all the other competitors and muttering under her breath.

"It's her!" Mia hissed. Grabbing Sita's and Violet's arms, she stared at the woman. "That's the woman I saw!"

"That's Mrs. Varley, Sadie's mom," said Violet.

"Don't come any closer!" Sadie's mom snapped as a mom and boy went over to see her sculpture. "Only the judges can come close. Go away!"

"She's acting really oddly," said Violet.

"Look at this one, Mom." The boy who had just been told to go away pulled his mom over to Alice's table. "This is definitely the best!"

Mia caught her breath as she saw a look of utter fury cross Sadie's mom's face.

"No!" Sadie's mom hissed to herself. "Mine's the best. Mine will win." She picked up some scissors.

"Quick!" Mia gasped, fear jolting through her. What if Sadie's mom did something awful? "We have to get those scissors. Oh, why isn't Lexi here?" Lexi could have used her super-speed to grab the scissors in a second.

"I know what to do!" Violet said, and she whispered Sorrel's name. The cat suddenly appeared. She looked around in surprise at all the people. Violet whispered something to her, and then they hurried toward Mrs. Varley. Sorrel leaped onto the table containing Mrs. Varley's structure.

"No!" Mrs. Varley gasped. "Get away, cat!" She dropped the scissors and started flapping her hands. Violet grabbed the scissors and pocketed them as Sorrel darted from one side of the sculpture to the other.

"I'll get it," said Violet, scooping Sorrel up. "I'm sorry!" She hurried back to the others, the scissors bulging in her pocket.

"It?" Sorrel hissed under her breath. "You called me *it*?"

"Shh," Violet whispered. People were already looking at them. "I'm sorry. She's my cat. I'd better take her home," she called to everyone.

Violet hastily left the parking lot with Mia and Sita.

"Good plan for getting the scissors," said Sita as they hurried back up the street.

"I thought Mrs. Varley was going to destroy someone else's sculpture with them!" said Violet. "The grown-ups are getting totally out of control! We have to find out where these Shades are, right now. If we can send them back to the shadows, then the hold they have will break, and everyone they're affecting will return to normal."

"Before anyone gets seriously hurt!" said Mia, her heart racing.

"I think we should go to Lexi," said Sita. "We need her."

Violet nodded. "Can you see where she is with your magic, Mia?"

Mia got out her mirror and looked into it.

"Lexi," she said.

An image formed. It showed Lexi in her bedroom, rattling the door handle. "Mom! Let me out!" she was shouting.

"No," Lexi's mother's voice came through the door. "You can stay in there and work on your math paper. Ninety-two percent is not good enough. You will do it again and get a hundred percent, and you can forget all about going out tonight!"

"Lexi's been locked in her room," Mia said. She saw Lexi fighting back tears as she slumped down on her bed.

Pulling out her phone, Lexi dialed a number. "Hi, Lizzie, it's me," she said a moment later. "I can't come over tonight." There was a silence. "I'm sorry, I just can't. It's my mom. She's making me do a ton of work…. No, I can't change her mind. She's being awful, Lizzie." Lexi's voice broke with a sob. "I'm feeling scared of her and…." She broke off, and then her shoulders slumped. "Okay. I get it, you've got to go. I'll see you Monday at school." She clicked the phone off and threw it down, and then buried her head in her hands and started to cry.

"We've got to go to her!" said Mia. It was horrible seeing Lexi so unhappy. "Maybe *her* mom is being affected by Shades, too. She's being full-on crazy!"

Violet ran to a patch of shadows under a tree at the side of the street with Sorrel bounding beside her. "Come on," she said, holding out her hands.

Sita and Mia ran and grabbed a hand each, and the next moment, they felt themselves spinning away.

11
STAR FRIENDS VS. SHADES

As their feet hit carpet, they heard a sharp intake of breath. Mia saw Lexi staring at them from her bed. "What are you doing here?" she demanded.

Mia squeezed out from the gap beside the wardrobe and went over to her. "Lexi, I'm really sorry…. I shouldn't have accused you of going to Lizzie's instead of meeting us."

"We are all sorry," said Sita, joining her.

"We want to apologize," said Violet.

"You should have known I wouldn't do

that!" said Lexi reproachfully.

"I know," said Mia.

"And we are all really, really sorry," said Violet. "But right now, there's other stuff going on that we absolutely have to deal with, and we need you!" She looked at the door. "Did your mom lock you in?"

Lexi wiped away her tears. "She's gone crazy. She wants me to redo a math paper, and I'm not allowed out until I get every question right. I don't know what's up with her!"

"It's a Shade," said Violet. "The Shades that are in Westport are making adults really competitive."

"It's why my mom wants to beat everyone in the fun run and why my dad has gone loopy over a family quiz," said Mia. "Oh, and also why Sadie's mom destroyed Mr. Jones's sculpture— she wants to win the beachcomber competition so badly. Just now we had to stop her from attacking someone else's sculpture with scissors!"

Lexi stared at her wide-eyed. "So it's not just my mom being a crazy control freak?"

"Nope," said Mia. "This is all because of dark magic, and we need to figure it out. Should we call the animals?"

"Yes," Lexi said. "Mom won't come back for a while. She thinks I'm doing the math paper." A look of relief crossed her face. "Thanks for coming. I was so upset with you all. I didn't think I wanted to see any of you, but really I did. I tried telling Lizzie how horrible Mom was being, but she just said she was busy and hung up."

Mia remembered the phone conversation she'd overheard. "So you were planning on seeing her *after* you met up with us?" she said.

"Yes, you'll always come first—you and magic. But I do have fun hanging around with Lizzie and the others, and I don't want to have to choose between you," Lexi said, looking upset.

Mia took a deep breath. "I shouldn't have said you had to." She realized she'd been guilty of being just as controlling as Lexi's mom and felt a rush of guilt. "You can be friends with Lizzie as well as us. It's fine."

Lexi smiled and hugged her. "Thank you, but you three will always be my best friends. And Juniper, too, of course! Now, let's call the animals and see if we can figure out what's going on!"

Soon, they were all sitting around on Lexi's bedroom floor trying to think what the three Shades might be trapped in. The animals cuddled up to the girls.

"We need to think of something that's in Mia's house, Lexi's house, and Sadie's house," Violet said. "What have you recently gotten?"

"We all bought stuff at *Fairy Tales*." Mia realized she had the friendship bracelet on and

held her arm out. "Here, does it smell like
Shades?"

"And what about the dragon egg I got?"
said Lexi, jumping up and getting it from her
desk.

Sorrel and Willow sniffed both, but then
shook their heads.

"So what else do you two have that's new?"
said Violet.

"The red hair clips Lizzie gave us!" Lexi
said, spotting hers on her desk. "What about
those?"

Mia shook her head. "No, I gave mine back to Lizzie." She thought back over the images she'd seen with magic. The hooded figure … the clearing … the bottles of potion … the crystals on the shelf with the colorful dreamcatchers behind them….

"Dreamcatchers!" she gasped. "Lizzie gave us dreamcatchers!" She stared at the others, her hands flying to her mouth. "Oh, no! I've been so silly! I thought the magic was showing me the crystals on the shelf at *Fairy Tales,* but it wasn't the crystals that were important; it was the turquoise and pink dreamcatchers hanging up behind them! I've got one, and so do Lexi and Sadie!"

"But Sorrel would have smelled Shades in them in *Fairy Tales*," argued Violet.

"There were definitely no Shades there then," said Sorrel.

"Elizabeth could have bought them before we went in," said Mia. "Don't you remember?

When we got there, Alice was restocking them!
She said they had been selling like hotcakes.
I bet Elizabeth had just been in and bought a
bunch of them, and the three turquoise and pink
ones had Shades in them."

"But why? Who put them there?" said
Juniper, jumping onto Lexi's bed in agitation.

"I don't know, but what's important now is
getting our hands on those three dreamcatchers
and sending the Shades back to the shadows
before one of the adults does something really
bad!" said Mia.

"Where's yours, Lexi?" said Sita.

"In the hallway outside my bedroom."

They looked at the locked door.

"How are we going to get it?" Mia said.

Lexi smiled. "Mom might have locked
me in, but there are other ways out of this
room than through the door!" She ran to the
window, opened it, and a second later was
climbing out. "Back in a minute!"

In fact, she returned in less than a minute, the blue dreamcatcher in her hand as she climbed back in through the window. She jumped down to the floor. "Here it is," she said, throwing it onto her rug.

Sorrel and Willow walked cautiously toward it but then both jumped back, Sorrel with a hiss, Willow with her nostrils flaring.

"Shade!" Sorrel spat.

"Are you sure?" Violet said.

"Without a doubt," said Sorrel.

"Yes. There's definitely a Shade in it," said Willow nervously.

"What do we do?" said Lexi.

"Sita, you command the Shade out from the dreamcatcher—it will have to do whatever you say—and then I will order it to go back to the Shadows," said Violet. She was a Spirit Speaker, a special kind of Star Friend who could banish Shades back to the Shadow World.

"Remember, you need to be looking it in the eyes to send it back to the shadows," Sorrel said.

"I know," Violet said impatiently. "But Sita can command it to look at me."

"Are you ready, Sita?" Mia said.

Sita took a deep breath. "I command you to come out, Shade," she said, staring at the dreamcatcher. "Show yourself."

For a moment nothing happened, and then a shadow seemed to move over the surface of the dreamcatcher. It swirled faster and faster, like a mini tornado, and then burst upward toward the girls and animals. As it did so, the smoke formed into a tall, thin shape with long arms, spiny fingers, sharp teeth, and red eyes. Mia felt a shiver run down her spine and saw Sita's face turn pale.

"Free at last!" the Shade hissed.

"I want you to freez—" Sita started to speak, but before she could finish commanding it, the Shade had leaped toward her. It clamped its hand over her mouth, stifling her words.

"Let her go!" Mia gasped as Sita struggled frantically in its grip.

"Oh, no." Its mouth widened into a gloating smile. "Did you think I couldn't hear you talking while I was in the dreamcatcher? I could hear every word. I know to avoid that one's gaze." It nodded at Violet while not looking directly into her eyes. "And I know that this one is dangerous. Well, she will not command me. In the catcher, I could only affect a few people. Now I am free, and I will go where I wish."

"To do what?" demanded Lexi.

The Shade smiled evilly. "To cause unhappiness and bring discord. I will talk to people in their sleep, bring them dreams that feed their ambitions, make them dream a future where they could win, and lead them to a point where they will hurt anyone who stands in their way," it sneered. "It is easily done. Whisper words in their ears, and soon their personality starts to change...."

"But only adults can hear you?" said Mia.

"Yes, only adults," the Shade agreed.

"Why would you do it?" said Lexi.

"Because every time I do something evil, I grow stronger," hissed the Shade.

Sita struggled under the Shade's hand.

"Let Sita go!" Mia said through gritted teeth.

"No," said the Shade. Mia and Violet both stepped toward it. "Stop there. If you come near me, I shall hurt her." It flexed its vicious fingernails and drew a faint line across Sita's neck. Pinpricks of blood welled up where his razor-sharp nails touched her skin.

Sita struggled desperately. "Stay still!" it snapped. "Or I shall do worse!" It looked at the others. "You are going to let me go free. If anyone tries to stop me, this girl will suffer." It edged away, its angular bones clicking as it dragged Sita with it. Mia knew they had to stop it! It couldn't be allowed to affect a bunch of people while getting stronger and stronger all the time. Her mind raced through all the things they could do. The only way to stop it was to free Sita so she could command it, but how could they do that? A plan suddenly came to her.

Using her magic, she saw the Shade's outline move a second before it made the move for real. Its hand was reaching for the window. "You're not going anywhere!" she cried, leaping forward and barreling into the Shade with her shoulder, knocking it away from the open window. "And if you want to hurt someone, you can hurt me, not Sita!"

The Shade lost its grip on Sita. She took the opportunity to tear herself free. With a snarl, the Shade grabbed Mia and slashed its hands at her. She gasped and ducked, hiding her face. She'd been ready for the pain—expecting it—but it still hurt. Its talons raked down her arm, and she cried out. Bracken snarled in fury and grabbed its leg while Juniper leaped at its head, Willow butted its arm, and Sorrel dug her claws into its foot, but the Shade took no notice. It lifted its hand. It was going to slash her face!

"Stop hurting Mia!" Sita shouted, scrambling to her feet. "Stop it now!" The Shade's hand froze in midair. It had to do as Sita commanded.

Pushing Mia away in disgust, it leaped for the window.

But Lexi reached the window first with her super-speed and slammed it shut. "You're not going anywhere!" she cried.

Sita stared at Mia. Blood was trickling from her arm. "What's it done to you, Mia?"

"Don't worry about me!" Mia said, holding the wound. "Just send it back to the Shadows!"

"I order you to face Violet!" Sita commanded.

The Shade tried to fight against the command, but Sita's power was too strong. Its body shook with anger as it reluctantly turned to Violet. She marched up to it. "You hurt Mia!" she said furiously.

The Shade glared at her. "I shall hurt you all!" it hissed.

"Oh, no, you won't," said Violet. "Your time here is done, Mr. Spiny Fingers. Go back to the shadows. I command it!"

The Shade's body started to dissolve in gray smoke. It faded faster and faster until the last few wisps of smoke chased each other in a circle and disappeared with a pop like water going down a drain.

"It's gone," said Lexi in relief.

"Oh my goodness, Mia." Sita threw herself

down beside her friend. "That was so brave. You saved me." Blood was seeping out from under Mia's fingers. "But look what it did to you."

"It's okay. You can use your magic to heal me," Mia said, gritting her teeth. "I knew we couldn't defeat it unless you were free."

"So you made it attack you instead," said Violet, her eyes wide. "That was really brave."

"Help Mia, please, Sita," Bracken begged.

Sita crouched down and looked at the wound the Shade had made with its nails. She put her hand just above the wound and concentrated hard. Mia felt a pleasant tingling sensation sweep over her skin. She watched as the blood dried up and the marks got smaller and smaller, shrinking to tiny scratches and then disappearing altogether, leaving her skin slightly pink.

The pain vanished. "You made it better!" she said, hugging Sita. "Thank you."

Bracken jumped around excitedly and licked Willow on the nose. Juniper raced across the curtain rod, and even Sorrel gave a satisfied purr.

"Now we need to get our hands on the other two dreamcatchers," Sita said.

They heard footsteps outside Lexi's room. "Lexi?" It was her mom.

The animals disappeared instantly. Violet gestured to Sita and Mia to go to the shadows beside the wardrobe with her.

"Wait. I'll try to get rid of her," Lexi whispered. "Yes?" she called to her mom.

There was the sound of a key turning in the lock, and the door handle moved. Lexi stepped out into the hallway, pulling the door shut behind her.

"Lexi, I'm sorry." Her mom sounded strained. "I don't know what came over me this afternoon. I should never have locked you in here, and making you redo that math paper for the sake of eight percent was a terrible idea. I have no idea why I said it. I've been feeling so strange the last few days. It's like I've had a voice in my head making me feel like it was really important that you did well. I was downstairs just now, and it was as if a cloud had suddenly cleared. I've been pushing you entirely too much. I'm sorry."

"Does this mean you're not going to make me do all those extra classes?" Lexi asked hopefully.

"No, you don't have to do them, and of course you can go and see your friends this afternoon."

"Thanks, Mom!" They could hear the smile in Lexi's voice. "I'll just get my things."

She shut the door, and the others stepped out from behind the wardrobe.

"Did you hear all that?" Lexi asked.

They nodded. "One dreamcatcher down, two to go!" Mia said.

First, Mia used her magic to see where Sadie's dreamcatcher was—it was hanging in her bedroom window—and then Lexi went downstairs and told her mom she was going to Mia's house.

The girls all met up outside and walked to Sadie's house. It was a detached house slightly set back from the road. Mia had seen that Sadie's room was on the top floor. There was a large tree outside it, and the window was slightly open.

"Sadie will be at Lizzie's, so we should be safe to get in," said Lexi. "I'll call Juniper, and he will help me. We'll climb the tree, and then he can get in through the window and pass the dreamcatcher to me."

While the others kept watch, Lexi raced to the house. They saw the branches of the tree move as she climbed up it, and then there was a blur of red as Juniper leaped from the branches onto the windowsill and vanished inside, reappearing with the purple dreamcatcher in his mouth. He gave it to Lexi, and she was back beside them in no time.

"Got it!" She grinned. "I can put it back later when we've gotten rid of the Shade!"

"Just mine to get now!" said Mia.

Not long afterward, the girls and their animals were staring at Sadie's and Mia's dreamcatchers on the floor in Mia's room.

"How do we do this?" said Lexi.

"I'll command the Shades to come out," said Sita confidently. "Only this time I'll be ready, and they won't get the better of us." She stared at the dreamcatchers. "Here goes. Shades, I command you to leave the dreamcatchers and to freeze as soon as you are out."

Gray smoke
swirled from the
dreamcatchers,
swirling faster
and faster as
it formed two
tall, thin shapes.

"Freeze
without saying
a word!" Sita
commanded.

The Shades froze where they
were, their red eyes open. They looked
terrifying, but they couldn't move or speak.

Violet pointed at them. "Oh, dear. We
spoiled your little game. Now, return to the
shadows!" she ordered.

The Shades' eyes flashed with fury, but they
had to obey, and they disappeared in a puff of
gray smoke.

"We did it!" cried Lexi.

Mia felt an overwhelming rush of relief. "I can't believe it." She looked around. "They're really gone."

"We're so awesome!" said Violet, high-fiving her. "It's all over!"

"Well, not really," Sita pointed out. "We still have to find out who trapped those Shades in the first place."

"Yes, and stop them from conjuring more Shades," said Mia.

Bracken jumped into Mia's arms. "I'm up for the challenge!"

Mia buried her face in his soft fur. "And me!" she declared. "But for now, I really need some food. I didn't have any lunch, and I'm starving."

"Me, too," said Lexi. "Mom didn't even give me a chance to have lunch."

"I'll get us some food," Mia said.

She went downstairs to the kitchen. Her mom was sitting at the table in her running gear, having a cup of tea.

"Are you going running, Mom?" Mia said, wondering how her mom would be now that the Shade was gone. People usually forgot everything that had happened when Shades returned to the shadows.

Her mom sighed. "I should, but I just don't feel like it anymore. I think I've been taking this fun run much too seriously." She held out an arm, and Mia went over. Her mom hugged her. "I've hardly seen you this week. Now, weren't you saying you'd like to go to The Copper Kettle the other day? How about we stop at the beachcomber competition to see who won, and then go to the café? I'll treat you, your friends, and Max to sandwiches, hot chocolate, and cake. How does that sound?"

"Awesome!" Mia said.

"Did someone mention cake?" Her dad put his head hopefully around the kitchen door.

"Yes, we're all off to The Copper Kettle," said Mia's mom.

"Count me in!" her dad said. "I am so tired of looking at all these quiz questions!" He crumpled up the paper in his hand and tossed it aside. "It's like I've had a voice in my head telling me to keep on practicing, keep on revising. It's even been there in my dreams. And what's it all for? It's going to be a good family fun night out, win or lose. No more practicing, that's what I say. Let's go out and eat cake!"

Mia grinned in delight. "I'll get the others!" she said.

They all piled into the Greenes' car. Mia's mom took a detour to the beach parking lot on the way to The Copper Kettle. The judging had just taken place, and Alice was beaming beside the first-place ribbon next to her sculpture.

"Great job," said Mia, going over to her. She felt awful now that she'd suspected Alice of being the person doing dark magic.

"Thank you, dear. I'm thrilled!" Alice winked and whispered, "Those little fairies in my yard did a very good job, didn't they?"

Mia smiled. She wished Alice would stop talking to her as if she were five years old, but she could see now that she meant well, and

it was just her way of
being friendly. Maybe
one day they would
get her to tell them
more about the plant
magic she did.

Sadie's mom
hadn't won anything,
but she didn't seem
to mind. "The winners
were all so good,"
Mia heard her saying. "I
enjoyed making my sculpture
anyway."

Even Mr. Jones seemed happy. He'd been
asked to help judge the competition, and
he was standing with the other three judges
laughing and joking as they had a cup of tea.
"Next year I'll be back with something even
better!" he was saying.

"You've got to give everyone else a chance

every once in a while," joked one of the other judges.

After looking at all the beautiful sculptures, Mia and the others set off for The Copper Kettle. The cozy café was warm inside, the air filled with the smell of cake and coffee beans.

"Mmm," said Mia, breathing in deeply.

"Hello, everyone," said Mary, the owner. "One table or two?"

"I'm sure the girls would rather sit by themselves if you've got space," said Mia's mom.

"Of course," said Mary. "No problem at all. Follow me, girls." She showed Mia, Lexi, Violet, and Sita to a large round table with comfy armchairs tucked away around the corner in an alcove, while Mia's mom and dad picked up some crayons and a coloring book for Max, grabbed a couple of newspapers, and sat down at a smaller table next to the window.

Soon they were all eating delicious tuna and

ham and cheese sandwiches with the crusts cut off, blueberry muffins, mini cupcakes covered with frosting, little chocolate brownies, and slices of apple and strawberries.

"This is the best meal ever!" said Lexi happily.

"We deserve it," declared Violet. "It's been a very busy day."

"A busy, *magical* day," said Mia. They all grinned. "I think I know some others who deserve a yummy meal, too," she went on. She nodded to the large table covered with a tablecloth. "There's plenty of food left," she whispered. "We could call the animals. If they hide under the table, no one will know they're here!"

The girls exchanged mischievous looks. They knew they shouldn't, but they all wanted to!

They checked that Mary was busy talking to a customer, and then they called their

animals' names. The four animals appeared
in a shimmer of light and looked around in
surprise.

"Quick! Under the table!" Mia whispered.
They all bounded under the tablecloth.

Soon, Bracken and Sorrel were eating
sandwiches while Willow ate the apple and
Juniper nibbled on a strawberry. The girls
could feel their soft bodies pressing against
their legs.

Mia slipped her hand under the table and
rubbed Bracken's fluffy head, feeling happiness
rush through her. They still had a lot to find
out, but right now, all that mattered was that
she was with her best friends and their animals,
and everyone was safe.

"This really *is* the best meal ever!" she said
with a smile.

About the Author

Linda Chapman is the best-selling author of more than 200 books. The biggest compliment she can have is for a child to tell her he or she became a reader after reading one of her books. She lives in a cottage with a tower in Leicestershire, England, with her husband, three children, three dogs, and three ponies. When she's not writing, Linda likes to ride, read, and visit schools and libraries to talk to people about writing.

About the Illustrator

Lucy Fleming has been an avid doodler and bookworm since early childhood. Drawing always seemed like so much fun, but she never dreamed it could be a full-time job! She lives and works in a small town in England with her partner and a little black cat. When not at her desk, she likes nothing more than to be outdoors in the sunshine with a cup of hot tea.

9
TROUBLE!

Mia arrived at school the next morning at the same time as Lexi. She could tell right away that her friend was not in a good mood by the way she was stomping up the path.

"What's up?" Mia asked, falling into step beside her.

"My mom!" Lexi threw her hands in the air. "I've tried telling her I don't want to do all the extra things she has planned, but she just keeps going on about how helpful it will be for my 'future career prospects' and says I'm doing the extra things whether I like it or not!"

"That's awful," said Mia sympathetically.

"She's so controlling!" Lexi burst out. "I want to come and meet you tonight, but she says I have to fit in more piano practice, and tomorrow she's taking me to meet my new flute teacher. Sita called me and told me what happened yesterday, and I know I need to be with all of you." Tears sprang into her eyes, and she blinked them away.

Mia hugged her. There wasn't much she could say. "We'll meet up Saturday at lunchtime like usual, as soon as you've finished gymnastics." She lowered her voice. "And try to track down the you-know-whos then."

"Lexi!" Lizzie breezed up with Sadie. She ignored Mia. "Do you want to come over to my house tomorrow night?"

"I can't," sighed Lexi. "I have a flute lesson."

"How about Saturday, then?" Lizzie said.